(sometimes people ask me if I write about them. maybe I do, maybe I don't. it's that simple, if my words speak to you, they are for you. maybe not in the first place, but they are.)

for everyone I've loved.

for those who broke my heart.

I took the tragedy and carved it

into places where it would stay.

for those who find more comfort in a book than in themselves.

for all those who are still fighting.

and everything that remains when we leave

are the scars in the hearts of those who loved us tenderly or wildly

and the trace of burnt soil on fields

that seemed to be crushed by the heavy grey fog before.

does the quiet calm you or does it tear you apart?

there is not that one thing that destroys you. it's just that when you go through hard times, you get a crack. and this is not bad at first, quite the contrary, through these cracks the light comes in and eventually they heal. but when life permanently drags you down, more and more cracks emerge and one ends up as a bunch of shards, despite all frantic efforts unable to fix oneself into the original shape. cause even if this works, the scars will remain; visible, ugly, aching, silent witnesses of all our failures. time does not bring relief and time does not heal all wounds, it just makes them fade a little.

- **why we are breaking apart**

this is to all the crooked young souls out there. to the kids who sit alone in the bus, hiding in their seats and to those who always laugh but feel alone in the crowds. to those who promise every cigarette will be their last and still smoke their lungs to death. to those who stay up all night because they are scared to sleep alone in cold and empty sheets. to those who always drink a few shots too much. to those who find more love in a book than they could ever find in themselves. to those who didn't think they'd make it to this year. to those who always expect a little too much and try a little too hard. to those who still fight and scream louder than the thousands of voices in their minds. to those with scars on their skin or in their hearts.

remember how often you thought that this night would be your last but you woke up the next morning. calm seas don't make good sailors, waves and hurricanes do. you will get through it, even if times are tough.

- **for the warriors**

the smell of smoke won't get off my hands, no matter how often I wash them. you won't ever get off my head, no matter how many lips touch mine.

you asked me, how do I define home? but what you didn't know is that the answer is you. before I got to know you, I was homeless, wandering through the cold and empty streets of this grey city. but then you came. the fire in your eyes enlightened my heart and I realized that home is not about four walls and a roof because I found mine in the taste of your lips and the smell of your hair and the touch of your hands on my skin and the way you look at me as if you see galaxies where I only see empty skies.

- **this house no longer feels like home**

and I could never leave you, cause it's like getting out of the hot bathtub which haunted the cold nothing out of my bones and pulling back over all those smoky black clothes of yesterday. all my scars fade when I'm with you and your touches make flowers bloom across my skin instead.

everything ends so fast,

withers and perishes

like a flower in the last autumn months.

the world turns so fast

and I can’t keep up with it anymore.

when your body is pressed against mine and still we are not close enough, when our minds collide and your love is pouring down on me like a thousand shooting stars, I realize that you're not my world, you are my universe. when you smile at me, the demons in my heart disappear and instead you fill it's thirst with the most beautiful flowers, grown on the ground of real true love and my weak little paperheart.

I remember the day, or should I say night, when I first saw fireflies. I can't tell why but I never saw one before in my entire life. we went to this party and I remember how we suddenly heard sirens of the police, which someone had been calling because the party probably was too loud. you took my hand and shouted "run girl!" and I ran.

retrospective I don't know why, but it felt right to run away, only because you told me to.

without knowing, we lead ourselves to a lake.
we sat there, not knowing what to do and I pulled a pack of cigarettes out of my pocket.

"you'll ruin yourself, darling", he said. but he never knew that he was ruining me like no cigarette in this world could.

we talked a lot and laid down on the warm asphalt and suddenly, the air around was flittering and fireflies floated above our heads and bodies like a thousand fallen stars.

after you left, I never saw one again.

when it comes to love, maybe the ocean is the best comparison. the sea fascinated me for my entire life, but so many times I almost drowned in it. these light blue waves transformed into tons of liquid grey cement, crushing my weak bones under its heavy weight. I promised myself never to fall in love again until the day I met you. your heartbeat was the lighthouse of my ocean, safely guarding me back to the coast, calming my waves with your smile, enlightening my depths with your eyes.

there is not much hope anymore and believing in miracles is for the weak ones and the dreamers. but how could one be a dreamer if I'm scared to go to sleep because everything I tried to suppress haunts me in the night, lying in those cold and empty sheets, drenched in sweat with eyes wide open and a heartbeat faster than a person as dead as me could ever have.

- **I'm not as good with words as I want to be and probably no one will ever understand how I feel at night**

people say, love appears when it's expected least. and so did you. you appeared and made the sun rise on my nightsky and turn all the blue and black into the softest shades of purple. when I am with you, I feel safe, like you are wrapping yourself around me, but not like just defending me, but protecting me from the inside and still giving me all the freedom I need.

I'm often moody and sad and I really don't deserve you, but you still look at me like I am everything you ever wanted.

you with your ocean eyes, messing up my inside every time our souls meet.

I hope we never grow apart.

"suffocate!"

is what I want to scream at the top of my lungs

but all I do is choking on tragedy myself.

and here you are, not in my heart but my heart itself. how is there a chance to love you and care for you when all I do is destroying myself and waiting for death while you are smiling at me and say that everything is going to be okay? my bonfire has come to its end and it's getting cold out here. save yourself, my heart, before my body turns into ashes and dust and you shatter reflecting the last flames of what we could have been.

sometimes you might get a cut. it heals. the dead skin drops off and you get new skin, but you haven't lost any part of you. you're still all there. here. and the particles of skin or whatever that drop off feed the ground again. so what I'm saying is that the world is us.

- **midnight conversation with a stranger**

once I was asked what comes to my mind when I think about starry heavens and oceans and it was the love between me and her. she is the nightsky, spangled with stars and I am the ocean.

I can be coloured in the lightest shades of blue and tempting for a touch on your skin. but under the surface, there are streams, riptides that swirl. constantly changing from calm to hell, I can drag anything down into the depth that previously was naive enough to venture in. whereas she is the starry heavens. millions of glowing and shining spots, infinite spaces and sometimes apparently so far apart. the starlit sky is so breathtaking beautiful, yet so unaware of it. infatuated by all those fake lights of the city, he feels pale and hideous. but when far out on the sea the night descends and the silence lays upon everything, the ocean and the starlit sky are on their own. the iriscendent black unifies and the stars are shining so bright that they enlighten the deepest depths and abysses of the ocean which on the other hand calms down and turns itself into a mirroring surface on which the starlit sky can finally see itself and perceive it's incomparable beauty.

getting close without

wanting all of you is hard,

but it is better than taking the solitude any longer.

watch me rip out the fire in my eyes

to enlighten candles along your spine.

but they burn down faster than I expected them to

and leave us in the darkness

with my eyes empty

and your body cold.

but kid, you got to love yourself. because in the end of the day the only home you have is your body and despite you hate it, don't set yourself on fire for a little warmth. it is your home and only yours and wounds may numb the pain for seconds but your scars will be an aching reminder of your pain forever. you will make it through this like you made it like through every other night before that you thought would be your last. the sun rose for you every dawn and this won't stop today.

In der Liebeslyrik aller Zeiten begegnet einem bei näherer Betrachtung fast unweigerlich der Satz „Ich würde für dich sterben“, sei es in Taten, gesprochen oder als Metapher. Ich hingegen möchte dir etwas anderes sagen, denn der Tod hat schon lange keine Bedeutung mehr. Wer tot ist, muss nicht mehr leiden und mit dem wirbelnden Karussell Schritt halten. Ich weiß nicht, ob ich genug Kraft hab und auch in Versprechen bin ich manchmal schlecht, aber ich möchte es trotzdem sagen und dafür kämpfen. Ich würde leben für dich.

this is to you and only you.

this is about the way your voice cracks when your smile breaks through your words.

this is about the way you look at me as if you saw artworks where I only saw a blank canvas.

this is about how your voice sounding like my favourite poem.

this is about the way you touch me, not skin on skin but soul on soul.

this is to us. the young, the wild, the reckless. the lovers.

while you are reaching for the stars
I'm writing poems about getting better
but to be honest I am not getting there
and my scars do not fade.

in the absence of everything I promise to hold your hand. and when the world comes crashing in, I promise to keep you safe. I won't hesitate to let you know what I feel for you and what you are to me. we were so young and naive but god, I fell for you the second I saw you. we made it through so many nights together, I was there when you couldn't sleep of fear and you were there when I broke down crying. and fuck yes, you broke my heart but I felt honored to get my heart broken by you. every time you tell me what I mean to you I realize that you're so worth all of this pain.

I'm out of my mind again. I took fourteen shots to forget your name but all it did was burning it into my flesh. I smoked too much to get your taste out of my mouth but it remains, remains, remains. you broke my heart with your white lies and your green eyes and all the words you whispered that I knew weren't made for a person like me. I hate you, I love you, I hate to love you and I fucking hate myself. may time bring relief, I hope you at least didn't lie about this."

- **you broke my goddamn heart and I broke down last night**

you will never burn me down again
for I have become the flames
arose from the ashes
I'm my own forestfire in no need of gasoline
I'm burning bright
I'll guide you through the night
and myself, too.

it's one of those days again. no matter how much I bleed, the demons still circle around in my veins. no matter how many pills wander through my chapped lips, nothing but obscure pictures and thunderstorms stay in my head. no lightning without deafening thunder. no matter how much I smoke, my lungs will never hurt as much as the crippling pain of solitude and a slow death by an overdose of life.

I've always been scared of falling in love because falling means hitting the ground, it means pain and broken bones and lakes of blood. You made sense of my mess and now I'm falling apart, I still see your halfbaked smile in the yellow lights of the trainstation, the way you pulled me close and you leaving me at the same place one week later. I let you in and you caved your name into my heart in the most beautiful and painful way possible. I knew you were a forestfire and you burned me down in between shots of vodka, starry nights and too many cigarettes. The evening you told me you didn't love me was alright and it was alright that you pulled me off the platform edge and by alright I mean terrible and I'm not fine at all. And most nights I lay awake wishing you were still with me and some nights I lay awake wishing I was dead. I'm scared it will never stop. I'm scared that it will always be you. You with your halfbaked smile and your green eyes.

- **falling in love and falling apart in may**

it's alright.

you don't have to stay

(awake).

this is what I told you

what I told you when

it was not alright

like I was the captain of our sinking ship

drowning

in a bottle

finding anything but oxygen at the bottom.

behind your lips there is the word "home" lying on your tongue, sleeping there silently soothing, waiting for it to quit your mouth to enter mine, haunting the demons out of my spine and goddamn, you make me homesick.

behind your eyelids there's a universe, much more than some kind of god could create, you ease all this pain and goddamn, you make me speechless.

I'm just so tired of fighting, a kind of tired that sleep won't fix anymore. I never really had you and now I'm torn apart, I'm collapsing and I'm dying and you don't even care, you never cared at all. white sheets, white-coated people are searching for some hint of colour in my thunderstorm called mind but all they find are stains of blood in books with wrecked up pages and the smell of your perfume still stuck in my shirt. you told me I should save myself but I'm weak.

Too weak to carry on, too weak to leave.

this is the first poem about you and maybe it's the last because sometimes I believe that you won't make it and you were right and I could break down on the platform edge with the thought on my mind of living without you. it's the first poem about you because in more than a year I didn't find a single word to describe the way you wear death in your eyes with this frightening kind of implicitness, the way you wear your heart on your wrists where wars took place and the thoughts in your mind. but above all that you are and all that you are not, you made me feel safe in a way that no one else had before. you, that's infinite understanding, my lighthouse in the darkest night. please, never leave me here alone.

for the first time I'm falling for the cure not the poison because my synapses burst under your light when I see you.

take me back to your bed, cover me under your sheet, you make these scars stop to bleed. you're enough of a proof of god for an atheist, with every word you speak my wounds start to heal. and most of the time that I feel fine it's because I'm looking in your eyes, I found comfort in you cause you're my greatest weakness and strength at the same time. the feeling of your skin on mine is whispering "you're safe here" and every kiss is screaming "I'm finally home".

if you're bleeding

you're not weak,

it's ok.

you're living,

breathing,

surviving all of this.

selflove might be your biggest revolution.

my therapist told me

she figured out my kind of dying

I don't want to be found

I disappear

and maybe this is the quietest form of suicide

when the bloodiest forms didn't work out

I watched you decay and be your own coffin that day late in november almost two years ago when you smiled back at me, all black to attend my own funeral, and I turned around at the end of the hallway, shaky hands clenched around a pack of gauloises, only to see you again.

day three out of psychiatry and I found comfort in this world at the mere sight of your face before I knew you would find hell in me when our bruised souls collided like lost planets orbiting through an empty universe.

drive your knife through my chest

I beg you

if you only lay down

roses at my grave once.

you should never crave to be seen
as the masterpiece of an artist
that everyone adores
and wants to hang up in their livingroom,
staring at it sobbing of pride with empty eyes.
be abstract art.
hide your pure blank canvas
under strokes of black and a gigantic mess
your beauty can only be seen
by those who look close,
those who really want to see you.

I wish I could sink my hands into my own flesh to rip out those demons which still clasp my spine so tight that my weak bones are breaking under the pressure. although I promise every cigarette will be my last, I still enlighten one after the other. what you don't know is that I smoke to choke the weeds that have been growing in my lungs for years. and when we lay in cold sheets at 3 am out of breath and with dizzy minds, you laugh at me and say that maybe I had a few shots too much. I will respond that it's okay and that I'm fine and my life is a long line of yes I am fine, but fine means terrible and I am so goddamn tired. may the sleep quickly lay upon my shaky eyelids and release my aching bones from a few fractures too much.

- **the things that no one will ever know**

I'm so scared to tell you how I feel
because you already left me once
because you thought you'd destroy me
but what you don't understand
is that I destroy myself
when you're not around
and the damage you do to me
is the loveliest pain I've ever felt.

but how am I supposed to fall asleep

when my demons never do

I could write sonnets to the way you lay your eyes upon me, don't get me started. It seems like they burst under all the love that cannot quit your lips, it drips out like honey or streams out like the wildest river under your pale eyelids directly into the deepest abyss of my soul. this is loving.

I could write novels about how I sink into your arms like the castaway sinks into the embracing sand of the shoreline. You pull me out of the black and blue and the metaphor of drowning means now longer dying but to be fulfilled by safety. this is healing.

I could write arias with my lips on your skin, tracing the small curve on your hip that you hate and kiss the scar on your hand that I hate cause its existence is my fault, but when you look at me and tell me you like it because its existence is a reminder of our reckless love, my love is pouring down on you like a thousand shooting stars. this is coming home.

who cares if you got honey spilling out of your lips

when your heart is poisoned

red lips, wide eyes

you were my apple

beautiful yet poisoned

and I was meant to die from the second I saw you

temptingly beautiful and deadly beyond all comparison

I took the biggest bite I could get

venoms circling in my veins

toxins rushing through my brain

you were so worth all of this agony

I think and collapse

dead lips, white lies

- **call me snowwhite**

and please, promise me this

I know you hate promises

but I need something to hold onto

since I'm scared of existence without you by my side

promise me that

you won't be leaving when I fall

I'm not lazy, I just can't get out of bed for the thirteenth day in a row.

I'm not dumb, I just can't handle the pressure that is put on me.

I don't want to be extraordinary, I just don't fit in to societies standards.

I'm not running away from responsibilities, I'm trying to escape myself.

how do you tell your parents that whilst you're grateful for their love there are days when you want to be anything but alive

on healing.

-allow yourself to sink.

-but force yourself not to drown.

-it takes time and the pain won't disappear, but you will get stronger.

-cry if you feel like it. plants don't grow without water once in a while.

-it might seem like you won't make it through this night, but remember how many times you thought this and you fucking made it.

-people care more about you than you think they do.

-being on medication doesn't make you weak.

-asking for help doesn't make you weak.

-you are beautiful.

-you are worth it.

-you are enough.

my skies turned into the softest shades of blue

and I realized that love was always only you

my mother knows I'm sick and so does my father by now, but it's still so hard to see them nervously looking at each other when I'm eating less or I can't make it out of bed or I come home after two bottles of the cheap sweet wine that makes you forget and even if I try to force a smile, the devil looks a lot like me those days.

I used to not care about who cares about me but when I see my mother holding back her tears and my father clenching his fist not knowing what to do of grief and despair and my brother seeing my blood at a way too young age it breaks my heart, I swear it does and I wish I could be alright from the deepest abyss of my heart.

- I'm sorry, I'm trying

you pour your love on me one second

and pretend I am nothing the other

maybe we were madly in love,

maybe just madly alone

and it's hard to admit

that we were never lovers

just the heroine in each other's veins.

don't you dare coming close and leaving me

when I let you in

despite all my fears.

don't you dare letting me down

when I'm aching, fighting, still breathing.

don't you dare making me feel like I'm not enough

because I am, for heaven's sake,

and if I am not good enough for you

I'm never ever going to choke again on all the shards

and broken pieces of my heart,

I'll spit them in front of your feet.

spring came and I was slowly recovering

the flowers grew back and began to bloom

in emptiest spaces

most hidden places

but now winter is returning and I am scared

they will die again

there's nothing tragically-romantic about a heart-break. there's nothing poetic about falling apart into a thousand pieces, unable to ever be in the same shape again because the scars will remain and ache. there's nothing beautiful about drowning in a black sea of sadness, crushed under layers of black water filling up your lungs. and every time I told myself that I'd find comfort in my pain I was lying because pain never made a home like two eyes and a heartbeat did.

- there's nothing poetic about falling apart

there's something I wanted you to know in the past year but what's the point anyways when someone else is making sense of your mess right now. you loved me in the best and purest way possible and I am so sorry, so fucking sorry for being a hurricane. and I want you to know that you couldn't have loved me better and you were so worth all of this torture. remember all our plans and dreams and hopes? they were always plans and dreams and hopes and they were everything but reality and I am so sorry, so fucking sorry for being a hurricane. even in hundreds of days spent together you'd never understand my kind of drowning and that was more painful for you than it will ever be for me. because you loved me, you loved me truly and there were miles in between falling in love and falling apart for you, but I crumbled and there was nothing separating these two.

even without fighting wars with blades on our wrists and drowning in each other, you couldn't have saved me because I'm already gone. looking at you makes it hard and some days I can't calm the voices in my head saying I lost you, I lost you, I lost you. I'm no longer the wind that makes the waves in the ocean. I want you to know that if it makes you feel better, I broke my own heart by losing you and choking on the shards, no matter if it was in crowded rooms or empty sheets, was way more painful than that.

- **to the girl with oceaneyes**

(I want to promise this is the last time writing about you but I can't)

I loved

and I loved

and I lost you

and I sent you through hell

only because I was afraid

to love you

and to lose you

so I left

lighter, chapped lips,

hit it one more time,

hit ***me*** *one more time, straight in the face,*

because our love was never kindness and softness

it was punchlines, fights and lakes of blood

but it was keeping me alive

how much weight of tragedy can a smile carry,

how many cracks can a heart be broken by and still beat,

how many unspoken words can the barriers called lips hold back

before you crumble, collapse and turn into your own supernova.

yes, I fear to lose you. cause you don't seem to understand what you mean to me and I feel deeply misunderstood when I tell you that you are the most beautiful being I have ever laid my eyes upon and you respond with nothing but a smile. I don't doubt on your love, how could I, when I only fall asleep fearless in your arms because I have finally, finally, found you. but it's not easy when you shut your words behind the barriers of your lips and I fear that I can never tear them down because all I have to offer is my weak little paperheart. most nights I lay awake it is due to the fear of losing you because you hate promises and all I want is you to stay but maybe I'm asking for too much.

- **what keeps me up at night (a question you never asked me)**

hearts were never meant to be

your greatest weakness

I guess I'll always be the girl

with a bottle pressed against her lips so tightly

like dead flowers between the pages

of her notebooks

and when you whispered to me,

nothing but millimeters, oxygen and real true love
parting our lips

the night we laid awake and stared into our eyes,

that you loved me more with every single flaw

I wanted nothing but to believe you

I wanted to talk to you the last few days. I wanted to tell you how I never forgot the way you made me feel. I wanted to tell you how my heart still skips a beat when I hear your voice and see your face in my dreams. don't get me wrong, I'm happy. but god, I loved you and believe me, I haven't moved past and you'll always have a piece of me.

I wanted to talk to you the last few days. I wanted to tell you how I'm smoking every cigarette thinking about you and what we could have been. I wanted to tell you that I miss your laugh. don't get me wrong, you hurt me like hell. but god, you made it feel like heaven and believe me, I haven't moved past and you'll always have a piece of me.

I'm so sorry that my hands shake when I run my fingers over your wrists where you fought battles no one could ever win

I'm afraid that we found forever at the wrong time

and that I poison your mind

like you shatter my heart

dear child of the sea

let me run back into your arms

like we ran across the cold sand this summer

catch me in your shoreline eyes and heart of gold

and let me stay until it's getting late

I don't care driving home at 2 am

being way too drunk

for every hour is not enough

because your presence is cure and your absence poison

we were never lovers and we will never be but we were lovers

in a way I never experienced it

lovers of nature and the sea and late night talks and alcohol and bad decisions

I promise to keep a part of how safe I felt this summer

and I'll remember your lighthouse smile

guiding me through the night until dawn

it's just me and the moon

it's just silence

although my inside is screaming the loudest

when I sit alone until dawn

and when the daylight breaks in

and the moon is getting paler

I wish to fade into the light of the rising sun, too

when I die bury me six foot deep
and don't you dare laying down roses on my grave
when you could never stand me aching
while I was still breathing

I always thought I'd fall for oceans

or forests

but no one told me

that I would find comfort

in a pair of sunset eyes

I don’t love like lovers do

neither with kindness nor with being soft

(maybe I do but I don’t want to seem like I need you because I do)

I love like a hurricane

beautiful yet painful

(mostly hurting myself by falling for the stronger storm)

and when I leave

there will remain broken bones and blood and the feeling that

you couldn’t carry the burden I warned you about

(and neither could I)

I hope that the day will come

where I don't see myself as the failure anymore

when things don't work out the way

I intended them to.

I ask myself why you love me.

how does a woman like you fall in love with a mess like me?

I mean look at you.

the way you enter a room and all the heads turn.

all eyes lay on you and I'm sorry that I feel the need to grab your hand

because it looks like I don't belong to you and I want everyone to know

that you might be their daydream, but you are my dream coming true.

I ask myself why you love me.

I am fulfilled with insecurities, too foolish at one time and

too weak when I cry in your arms and too strong when I hold my feelings in,

not daring to tell you what shakes up my inside,

afraid that you get tired of me collapsing.

I ask myself why I love you.

you tell me about how beautiful your evening with another woman was

and even though you don't look at her the way you sometimes look at me before we fall asleep,

it hurts my head.

you are the most beautiful rose to me

but your silence is made of thorns

and they are stabbing me while I try to hold you close and you run from me

I don't want to trim you but I'm afraid you will bloom even more beautiful in my absence

and the soil of love I give to you will no longer be enough.

I ask myself why I love you

when I write letters and poems and arias on paper or on your skin with my fingers

and you make me feel like a burden and only come to see me once in a while

don't apologize, I know that you don't have much time

I just want to feel like a priority sometimes.

maybe this is harsh to say but sometimes I can't fall asleep because I feel lonely lying next to you and I fear you will never understand what I feel.

I look for the answers to hold on to them, but deep down I know the answers as well as our loves worth

and all I can say that despite your fears and me lying awake every night

you are enough for me and I love you

and I hope you can say the same.

maybe I’m my own coffin every time

I search for forever in temporary people

sure I have felt heartbreaks prior

but you taught me without breaking my heart,

only by loving me and yet never caring enough

never asking if I got home safely

or why I cried myself to sleep last night,

you taught me that there sometimes

is no difference

in between spelling love and pain.

my biggest fear was never facing my own death

but that those I love could leave before I do

and it keeps me up at night to know that

if they are not here anymore

there is less sense in breathing than ever before

this is not a love poem.

this is about all the things that want to quit my lips, all the words I am whispering when you lay next to me sleeping and I'm awake and full of fear and love at the same time.

this is not the almost poem.

this is to us, the lovers. we made it this far and despite all our fears I found a safe harbor in your arms and maybe you can one day tell me that you feel the same.

this is not only about being soft.

it's to the scar on your hand and those on my wrists that you didn't cause but which remind you of how fragile I am.

it's about crying silently into my hands because I know the way you drive your car and I thought this time you wouldn't make it home.

this is not the home poem,

well maybe it is because of the way you look at me.

this is not screaming "I've searched for you all my life" because love came around when no one expected it to in a crowd full of people, making me hopelessly fall for you in the first place with our beers chugged too fast, too many cigarettes and sore hearts that lost all faith in love.

this is not a love poem

because it's the most bittersweet
ineedyouwithallmyheartpleaseneverleave
I've never spoken out loud.

and I guess I fall for girls that are cigarette breaks

or forestfires

but what's the point anyways

when they are burning you out

I always wondered why there is the word art in heartbreak

but when I saw myself bleeding out all of my pain into poems,

I understood.

don't you dare telling me my daylight is not bright enough. that my smile and the sparks of honey in my eyes are not beautiful and my warmth is not enough to comfort you through the night.

because I believed you.

I just wanted to be enough for you, be enough one last time so I took everything I had, bleeding out into the most beautiful sunset this world had ever seen. burning skies that marked my own downfall, only to see you staring at me with endless love and fascination like you did after we kissed for the first time.

there is nothing left and I hope you spend this night begging on your knees for the morning to come. I won't come back tomorrow to rise for you. I died for you one time and never again.

I guess you should leave

when you're in love

for the sake of not being alone

try not to push me away.

me, who found love in your hopelessly sore heart.

you tell me you lost faith in love and sometimes I want to scream into your face that you make me lose it, too, but instead I wrap you in my arms and tell you that we'll make it.

me, who takes you back after all the little things you say that hurt like hell but I tell myself that you didn't mean it this way and that it's alright. I forgive you every time.

I don't want you to leave but I guess one day you'll do. I'm fucking afraid when I look into your past and see the person you loved in the first place but left for no goddamn reason. maybe she wasn't enough. maybe I won't be either.

but let me assure you one thing, you'll never find someone that will love you the way I did. and I hope that you will remember the sound of my voice and the pure love in my eyes when you lose yourself.
I hope you get homesick.

all I want is to live at my fullest

be fulfilled, fall in love truly, pack my bags and leave this town that makes me suffocate

but all I do is coping

being a little to fulfilled with the cheap wine, falling apart and suffocating in this town

Wenn ich gehe, habe ich meinen Namen tief in deine rechte Herzkammer geschnitten. Und mit jedem Tropfen Blut, der durch deinen Körper pumpt, wirst du mich spüren. Ich werde ganz nah sein, solange dein Herz schlägt. Trag mich in dir, wie einen zarten Hauch, wie den Geruch einer kleinen Blume, der eben noch vor deiner Nase schien. Deren Geruch, den du wieder riechen willst, weil es dein Herz in erinnernde Melancholie hüllt. Wenn du mich vermisst, sei sicher, ich werde bei dir sein. Denn Fingerabdrücke, die man auf Herz und Seele der anderen hinterlässt, verblassen nie.

one of the things that scare me most is

that you can tell a person what you have been through and how it almost killed you

and they will put you through it again

I saw you in my dreams, darling (I can't sleep a single night without nightmares)

and it felt like home to see your face (and like hell waking up alone)

I can't wait to hear your voice again (because you did not call me last night when I needed you)

we could talk about the weather or you could spill over of drunk memories you want to tell me

(and it's alright I will listen, being quiet will hide where my voice would crack)

I hope you come back home soon, I love you
(I hope you make this emptiness disappear, I hate myself)

- solace in hell

note to my younger self.

pretending like it doesn't hurt, acting like you don't care won't make it pass.

it's 2 in the morning and my wounds start to bleed again

and your eyes speak in a foreign language I long to learn

and when I began circling

on my nineteenth lap around the sun

the earth I have been living on all my life

suddenly seemed a little less colder

and I saw a little hope

in my mother's eyes when I told her

that from now on

I'd try my best

not only to survive

but to live

take me out tonight

and while you're admiring art I'll do it in my own way,

dizzy by a few glasses of wine or completely sober, it does not matter,

either way I'll stare at you

like people do at sunsets

I defined home as people who tore me apart
and that's when I realized that home wasn't them,
it's me.
home is
the battlefield on my skin hidden under sleeves
soil brown eyes with drops of honey
messy hair
constellations of freckles on my lips
bony hips and bruised knees
a hurricane mind
and a paperheart.
It's okay to love wildly
but most important is that
I belong deeply to myself.

one day you won't be eighteen anymore. you will jump into your car and leave the town that used to make you feel like you were suffocating for years. you won't think about the girl with the green eyes and halfbaked smile anymore who broke your heart in this night in may.

you will no longer be the girl that's clenching her shaking fingers on a cigarette or the girl who kissed more bottles than humans or the girl that breaks down crying on her bathroom floor once in a while. you'll look back and realize that the worst is over and the best is yet to come. and all that will remain are memories with no longer a bitter taste to them.

- **you won't be eighteen and struggeling for the rest of your life**

you had my mind in your hands, you wandered through the hollow chambers of my heart, tasted life's bitterness and got drunk on love like I did.

handle my mind written on paper with care, for I am fragile.

the end.

I am Alaska (and no, I was not born with this name), the author. by the time this book is published I have almost finished my nineteenth lap around the sun. I am the girl that's always a little too awkward, that finds so much comfort in records and rainy autumn days and red wine (the cheap and sweet one that makes you dizzy but gives you a headache on the next day) and call it naïve but I still believe in real true love, after all that has happened. this book collects almost four years of falling in love and falling apart and my best attempts of healing which I'm doing, slowly.

If you want to get in touch with me, follow me on:

Instagram: https://www.instagram.com/solitudae

Tumblr: https://solitudae.tumblr.com

or write to my mail address: letterstosolitudae@gmx.de

Impressum:

Texte: © Copyright 2017 by Julia (Alaska) Schuele

Umschlaggestaltung: © Copyright 2017 by Julia (Alaska) Schuele

Umschlagsgrafik: © Copyright 2017 by Anna-Lena Benedix

Profilbild: © Copyright 2017 by Juliane Knapp

Verlag: Julia Schuele

73614 Schorndorf

Deutschland

letterstosolitudae@gmx.de

Druck: epubli – ein Service der neopubli GmbH, Berlin

Druck:
Canon Deutschland Business Services GmbH
im Auftrag der KNV-Gruppe
Ferdinand-Jühlke-Str. 7
99095 Erfurt